THE BLUE COCONUT

Thank you for your purchase from The Blue Coconut!

Advent Calendar Ages 8+

Welcome to Your North Pole Adventure!

We're thrilled to bring the magic of the North Pole into your home this holiday season! With our Christmas escape room adventure, you'll be guiding your child through a series of festive challenges and puzzles, each leading them closer to helping Santa prepare for Christmas Eve. Each day, there's a new puzzle to solve, a story to uncover, and a magical moment waiting to be shared.

This pack includes everything you need to create an enchanting daily experience throughout December. From coded messages to imaginative puzzles and clues, each activity helps build a special holiday story that's personalized and unforgettable. With themed challenges, creative story elements, and all the details for a seamless experience, you'll have everything at your fingertips to make this countdown to Christmas extraordinary.

Imagine the excitement as your child solves each day's puzzle, with you as their guide, adding magic and wonder with a new chapter of Santa's story. Your child will feel like a true adventurer, working alongside Santa's elves, helping Santa with his preparations, and perhaps even earning a special place on Santa's team!

Let's get ready for a holiday adventure filled with wonder, discovery, and festive fun!

How It Works:

1. **Daily Challenge:** Each day offers a unique puzzle or challenge for your child to solve. For younger children, we provide extra instructions and hints to help you guide them, ensuring they still experience the joy and sense of accomplishment that comes from solving the puzzle on their own. Once they finish, you'll have a special story extension to read, revealing the next part of Santa's magical journey. On some days, you'll also give them an object to keep until the big finale.
2. **Story Extensions**: After each puzzle is solved, read the story snippet provided. This adds depth and continuity to the adventure, making each day feel like a new chapter in a magical Christmas tale.
3. **Building Anticipation**: This adventure builds excitement as Christmas Eve draws closer. Your child's progress through the puzzles leads them on a journey from the North Pole workshop to Santa's sleigh, ending with a thrilling Christmas Eve finale.

Thank you for joining us on this journey. Let's bring some Christmas magic to your home together!

Preparation for Your North Pole Adventure

Before starting the daily puzzles with your child, a little preparation can make this journey even more magical and seamless! Here's what to do:

1. **Print the 'Advent Pack'**: Print out the full "advent pack' of daily puzzles, each labeled with the date, so it's easy to give the right challenge each day.

2. **Assemble the Codex Wheel for older kids they can do this themselves**: Follow the instructions provided to put together the codex wheel—this will be needed for certain puzzles. (We will guide you on when to provide this)

3. **Cut out the 'Extra Items'**: These items will be handed to the children on specific days. Keep an eye on the instructions to know when to share each item.

4. **Familiarize Yourself with the Info Pack**: Take a moment to read through this pack before Advent begins. You don't need to print it, but you'll want to refer to it daily to help guide your child's adventure and make the most of the escape room experience.

5. **Create a Supply Kit**: In addition to the puzzles, your child will need some basic supplies to complete activities. We suggest preparing a small kit with:
   - Scissors
   - Coloring pencils, pens, or crayons
   - A pencil
   - Eraser
   - Ruler
   - Counter or Small Coin
   - Glue (optional)
   - A notebook or scrap paper for notes and workings
   -

6. **Preview the Puzzle**: Before each day's activity, try completing the puzzle yourself. This will give you insight into the challenge and allow you to offer gentle hints if your child needs guidance.

7. **Preparation for Younger Children:** We provide an 'Elf Tip' each day for younger children; I recommend reading these out as part of the introduction. For very young players, under 8 we do offer a differentiated version of this pack which may be more suitable as some puzzles have be swapped to make them easier.

8. **Extra Tip for Familiarity with Christmas Songs:** Later in the game, one challenge involves recognizing four famous Christmas songs. If your child isn't familiar with these songs, consider playing them during earlier days to build familiarity with the titles and tunes. The songs are *O Christmas Tree*, *Little Donkey*, *Jingle Bells*, and *I'm Dreaming of a White Christmas*.

9. **Preparation of Extra Items:** You can add to the in-game items with small physical gifts, cookies or chocolates for a more interactive experience. Here are some suggestions for each:

- **Red Bauble Ornament/Cookie** - Write the number "3" on it.
- **Green Tree Ornament or Cookie** - Write the number "8" on it.
- **Basketball, Bouncy Ball, or Orange Cookie** - Mark it with the number "6."
- **Yellow Crystal Substitute** - Such as a chocolate coin or a small yellow treat or jewel-like candy with a "3" written on it; a cookie could work well if decorated with yellow icing.
- **Gingerbread Man** - Write the number "9" on it.
- **Pink Glove or Pink Cookie** - Mark it with the number "4."
- **Purple Gift** - Write the number "1" on it; it can contain any small treat or simply be a decorated cookie.
- **Blue Cookie** - Write the number "5" on it.

Now that you're prepared, you're ready to begin this magical journey to the North Pole. Each day holds a new adventure, bringing Santa one step closer to being ready for Christmas Eve. Enjoy every moment, and let the festive magic begin!

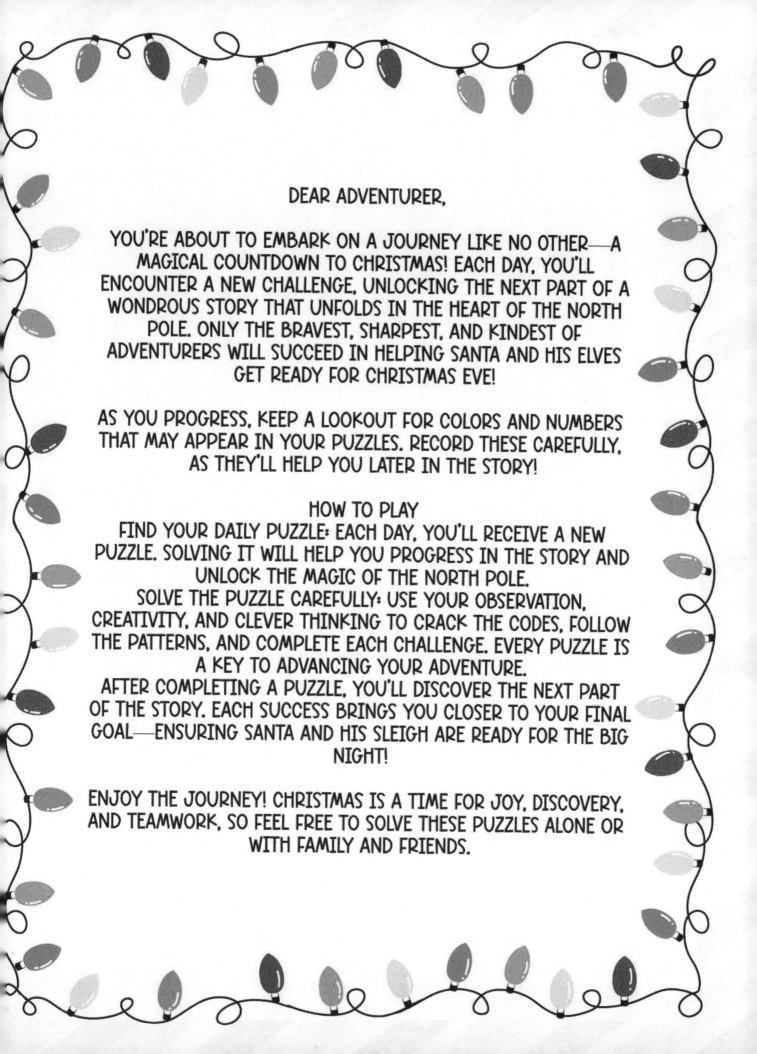

DEAR ADVENTURER,

YOU'RE ABOUT TO EMBARK ON A JOURNEY LIKE NO OTHER—A
MAGICAL COUNTDOWN TO CHRISTMAS! EACH DAY, YOU'LL
ENCOUNTER A NEW CHALLENGE, UNLOCKING THE NEXT PART OF A
WONDROUS STORY THAT UNFOLDS IN THE HEART OF THE NORTH
POLE. ONLY THE BRAVEST, SHARPEST, AND KINDEST OF
ADVENTURERS WILL SUCCEED IN HELPING SANTA AND HIS ELVES
GET READY FOR CHRISTMAS EVE!

AS YOU PROGRESS, KEEP A LOOKOUT FOR COLORS AND NUMBERS
THAT MAY APPEAR IN YOUR PUZZLES. RECORD THESE CAREFULLY,
AS THEY'LL HELP YOU LATER IN THE STORY!

HOW TO PLAY
FIND YOUR DAILY PUZZLE: EACH DAY, YOU'LL RECEIVE A NEW
PUZZLE. SOLVING IT WILL HELP YOU PROGRESS IN THE STORY AND
UNLOCK THE MAGIC OF THE NORTH POLE.
SOLVE THE PUZZLE CAREFULLY: USE YOUR OBSERVATION,
CREATIVITY, AND CLEVER THINKING TO CRACK THE CODES, FOLLOW
THE PATTERNS, AND COMPLETE EACH CHALLENGE. EVERY PUZZLE IS
A KEY TO ADVANCING YOUR ADVENTURE.
AFTER COMPLETING A PUZZLE, YOU'LL DISCOVER THE NEXT PART
OF THE STORY. EACH SUCCESS BRINGS YOU CLOSER TO YOUR FINAL
GOAL—ENSURING SANTA AND HIS SLEIGH ARE READY FOR THE BIG
NIGHT!

ENJOY THE JOURNEY! CHRISTMAS IS A TIME FOR JOY, DISCOVERY,
AND TEAMWORK, SO FEEL FREE TO SOLVE THESE PUZZLES ALONE OR
WITH FAMILY AND FRIENDS.

THE MAGIC OF THE SNOW GLOBE

It's December 1st, and as the first flakes of snow fall, you receive a mysterious, shimmering snow globe from an unknown sender. The snow globe feels warm in your hands, and as you gaze into it, you see a glimpse of Santa's Workshop at the North Pole, bustling with elves preparing for Christmas.

Suddenly, the snow globe begins to glow brighter, and you hear a tiny voice inviting you to join them!

"Solve this first puzzle," it says, "and be transported into a world of wonder. Only by helping us each day can you ensure that Christmas will be merry for everyone around the world!"

So, with excitement in your heart and a twinkle in your eye, you accept the challenge. Your adventure to the North Pole begins now!

As you gaze into the snow globe, you see a flurry of snowflakes swirling within. But something magical is hidden among them...

Your Challenge:
Among the snowflakes in the globe, only two are identical. These matching snowflakes hold the magic needed to transport you to the North Pole.
Once you find the matching pair, you'll be whisked away to the North Pole, where the next part of your adventure awaits!
Good luck, Adventurer!

P.S. We left you a bonus challenge on the base of the snow globe. Use your codex wheel to decipher it!

NAVIGATING THE NORTH POLE

You've arrived at the North Pole! The snow is deep, and the icy wind swirls around you. In the distance, you see faint lights and hear the jingling of bells—it must be Santa's workshop! But you'll need to figure out which direction to take.

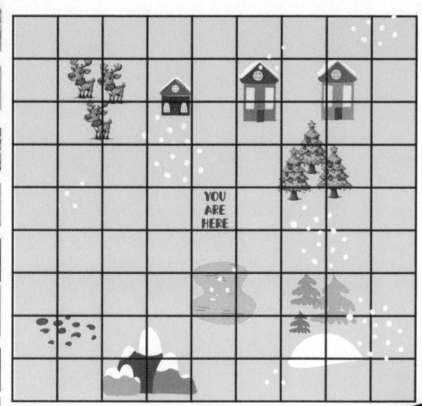

YOU ARE HERE

Your Challenge:
To reach Santa's workshop, you must find the right direction.
As you arrive in the North Pole, the night sky is filled with stars. An elf points to the constellations and says, "These holds the key to finding Santa's workshop! Solve the puzzle and it will show you the way. Look for the pattern hidden within the stars of the constellations. Once you solve the puzzle, follow the directions on the map and you'll uncover the location of Santa's workshop!

1   2
4   3

THE ENCHANTED WOODLAND

With the constellation code solved, you set off in the direction of Santa's workshop, feeling a renewed sense of excitement. After a while, the snowy landscape gives way to a dense, mysterious woodland. The trees are tall and covered in thick layers of snow, and twisting paths wind through the forest.

Just as you take your first steps inside, you hear a faint whisper. It's the wind through the trees, almost as if it's guiding you. But the forest is confusing, and many paths look similar. It would be easy to get lost can you safely make it through the enchanted woodland with the magic of Christmas is guiding your way!

CROSSING THE FROZEN LAKE

AFTER CAREFULLY FINDING YOUR WAY THROUGH THE ENCHANTED FOREST, YOU ARRIVE AT THE EDGE OF A VAST, FROZEN LAKE. THE ICY SURFACE GLISTENS IN THE WINTER SUN, BUT YOU NOTICE THAT SOME AREAS ARE TOO THIN TO STEP ON SAFELY.

BESIDE THE LAKE, YOU FIND A SIGN WITH A SERIES OF CLUES TO GUIDE YOU ACROSS. USING THESE CLUES AND THE MAP OF THE LAKE, CAN YOU DECODE THE COORDINATES TO REVEAL THE SAFE PATH? FOLLOW EACH CLUE CAREFULLY, AND YOU'LL MAKE IT ACROSS WITHOUT FALLING THROUGH THE ICE.
WITH THE RIGHT STEPS, YOU'LL BE ONE STEP CLOSER TO SANTA'S WORKSHOP!

DAY 4

(5th) ENTERING SANTA'S WORKSHOP

AFTER CAREFULLY NAVIGATING YOUR WAY ACROSS THE FROZEN LAKE, YOU ARRIVE AT THE GRAND DOORS OF SANTA'S WORKSHOP! THEY'RE TALL, BEAUTIFULLY DECORATED, AND LOCKED UP TIGHT. JUST AS YOU'RE WONDERING HOW TO GET INSIDE, A FRIENDLY ELF WITH A SPARKLE IN HIS EYE APPEARS AT THE DOOR. HE SMILES AND SAYS, "ONLY THOSE WHO CAN COMPLETE A CHRISTMAS TASK MAY ENTER! WE'RE PREPARING GIFTS FOR CHILDREN ALL OVER THE WORLD, AND WE COULD USE SOME EXTRA HANDS. IF YOU HELP US FIND THE MISSING NUMBER, I'LL GIVE YOU THE MAGIC PASSCODE TO UNLOCK THE DOOR."

YOUR CHALLENGE: FIGURE OUT WHICH NUMBER IS MISSING FROM OUR MAGICAL KEYPAD. USE YOUR OBSERVATION AND PROBLEM-SOLVING SKILLS TO UNCOVER THE ANSWER. ONCE YOU SOLVE THE TASK, THE DOORS TO THE WORKSHOP WILL SWING OPEN, AND YOUR JOURNEY INSIDE WILL CONTINUE!

DAY 5

THE MAGICAL TOY SORTER

YOU'VE MADE IT PAST THE GRAND DOORS OF SANTA'S WORKSHOP, AND THE PLACE IS BUSTLING WITH ACTIVITY! TOYS, GAMES, AND GADGETS ARE ZOOMING ALONG CONVEYOR BELTS, WHILE ELVES ARE BUSY PREPARING FOR CHRISTMAS EVE. SUDDENLY, YOU NOTICE AN ELF FRANTICALLY TRYING TO REARRANGE SOMETHING ON A PANEL. HE SIGHS IN RELIEF WHEN HE SPOTS YOU. "OH, THANK GOODNESS YOU'RE HERE!" HE SAYS. "OUR MAGICAL TOY SORTER IS ACTING UP, AND IT'S IN CHAOS! THE CONTROL PANEL IS A PICTURE OF SANTA AND HIS REINDEER, BUT IT'S ALL JUMBLED UP. IF YOU CAN PUT THE PICTURE BACK IN THE CORRECT ORDER, THE TOY SORTER WILL WORK PROPERLY AGAIN. ONCE IT'S FIXED, I'LL LET YOU TAKE A PEEK AT THE REST OF THE WORKSHOP FLOOR!"

YOUR CHALLENGE:
THE TOY SORTER'S CONTROL PANEL IS A PICTURE PUZZLE OF SANTA AND HIS REINDEER, BUT THE PIECES ARE ALL MIXED UP. REARRANGE THE PIECES TO RESTORE THE PICTURE. ONCE THE IMAGE IS COMPLETE, THE TOY SORTER WILL RESUME ITS MAGICAL SORTING, AND YOU'LL BE READY TO EXPLORE DEEPER INTO SANTA'S WORKSHOP!

NXSOGI AER

THE MISSING
NAUGHTY AND NICE LIST

AT LAST, YOU STEP INSIDE SANTA'S BUSTLING WORKSHOP! THE PLACE IS FILLED WITH BUSY ELVES, JINGLING BELLS, AND TOYS IN EVERY CORNER. THE SCENT OF PEPPERMINT AND GINGERBREAD FILLS THE AIR AS YOU LOOK AROUND IN AWE.

SUDDENLY, YOU'RE APPROACHED BY THE HEAD ELF, WHO LOOKS A BIT FLUSTERED. "OH DEAR, OH DEAR!" HE EXCLAIMS, WRINGING HIS HANDS. "I WAS HELPING WITH TOY PRODUCTION AND I SEEM TO HAVE MISPLACED SANTA'S NAUGHTY AND NICE LIST! WITHOUT IT, SANTA WON'T KNOW WHO TO DELIVER PRESENTS TO!"

HE GIVES YOU A HOPEFUL LOOK. "WOULD YOU BE ABLE TO HELP ME FIND IT? I LAST HAD IT WHILE WORKING ON TOYS, SO IT MUST BE SOMEWHERE AROUND HERE." CAN YOU HELP SEARCH THE WORKSHOP CAREFULLY AND LOCATE THE MISSING NAUGHTY AND NICE LIST. CHRISTMAS EVE PREPARATIONS CAN'T CONTINUE WITHOUT IT, SO EVERY SECOND COUNTS!
GOOD LUCK, AND REMEMBER, THE MAGIC OF CHRISTMAS IS ON YOUR SIDE!

LIGHTING UP THE WORKSHOP

YOU'VE SUCCESSFULLY FOUND SANTA'S NAUGHTY AND NICE LIST, BUT THE WORKSHOP IS STILL DIM AND NEEDS A BURST OF LIGHT TO BRING IT TO LIFE. THE MAGICAL LIGHT THAT POWERS THE WORKSHOP SEEMS TO HAVE WEAKENED, AND ONLY A SPECIAL CRYSTAL CAN REIGNITE IT!

YOUR CHALLENGE:

IN FRONT OF YOU, THERE'S A CIRCUIT BOARD WITH MULTIPLE COLORED CRYSTALS AND MIRRORS ARRANGED ON IT. EACH CRYSTAL HAS THE POTENTIAL TO POWER THE WORKSHOP'S MAIN LIGHT, BUT ONLY ONE CRYSTAL WILL DIRECT THE LIGHT BEAM CORRECTLY TO FILL THE WORKSHOP WITH A FESTIVE GLOW. THE CRYSTALS HAVE COME LOOSE, SO YOU NEED TO FIND THE CORRECT ONE TO PUSH BACK INTO PLACE. USE MRS. CLAUS'S KITCHEN AS A GUIDE AS THE KITCHEN LIGHT IS STILL FUNCTIONING, OBSERVE HOW THE LIGHT BEHAVES WHEN IT HITS A MIRROR TO HELP GUIDE YOUR CHOICES. ONCE YOU'VE FOLLOWED THE PATH AND FOUND THE CRYSTAL THAT COMPLETES THE CIRCUIT, PUSH IT INTO PLACE TO LIGHT UP THE WORKSHOP.

IMPORTANT: MAKE NOTE OF THE CRYSTAL'S COLOR AND THE LIGHT SWITCH NUMBER YOU USE TO ACTIVATE IT. THIS INFORMATION WILL BE ESSENTIAL LATER IN YOUR JOURNEY.

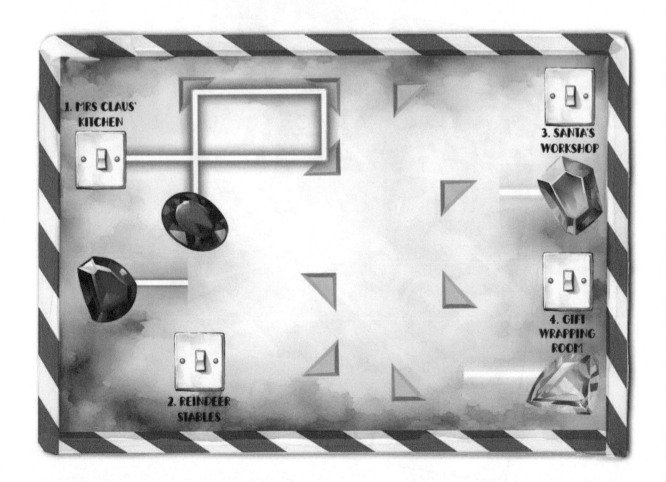

FIXING THE CONVEYOR BELT

NOW THAT THE WORKSHOP IS FILLED WITH LIGHT, YOU CAN SEE EVERYTHING CLEARLY. THE ELVES ARE BACK AT WORK, SORTING AND PACKING TOYS... BUT SOMETHING ISN'T QUITE RIGHT. ONE OF THE CONVEYOR BELTS HAS GROUND TO A HALT!

UPON CLOSER INSPECTION, YOU NOTICE THAT ONE OF THE GEARS IS MISSING A PIECE. SCATTERED ACROSS THE WORKSHOP FLOOR ARE SEVERAL GEAR PARTS OF DIFFERENT SHAPES AND SIZES. IF YOU CAN IDENTIFY THE CORRECT PIECE TO COMPLETE THE BROKEN GEAR, YOU'LL BE ABLE TO GET THE CONVEYOR BELT UP AND RUNNING AGAIN, ALLOWING THE ELVES TO CONTINUE THEIR WORK PREPARING TOYS FOR CHRISTMAS EVE!

ONCE YOU'VE ADDED THE MISSING PIECE, YOU'LL NEED TO TURN THE HANDLE ON THE RIGHT TO START THE MACHINE. WHICH WAY WOULD YOU TURN IT TO MAKE THE CONVEYOR BELT MOVE FORWARD TO THE RIGHT?

DAY 9

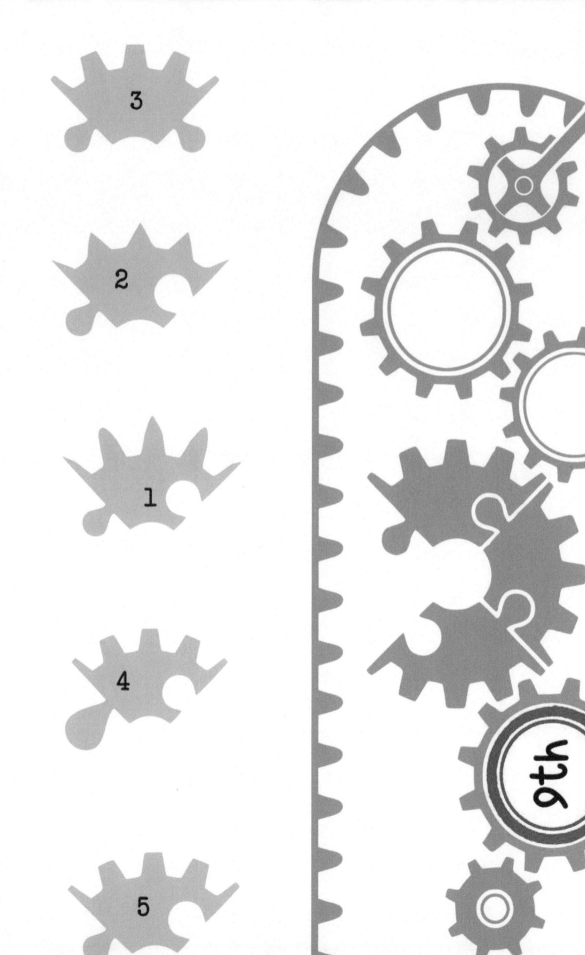

A VISIT WITH MRS. CLAUS

AFTER ALL YOUR HARD WORK IN THE WORKSHOP, YOU DECIDE TO TAKE A WELL-DESERVED BREAK. FOLLOWING THE DELICIOUS SMELL OF SPICES AND COCOA, YOU FIND YOURSELF IN THE COZY KITCHEN, WHERE MRS. CLAUS IS BUSY BAKING. SHE GREETS YOU WARMLY, HANDING YOU A STEAMING MUG OF HOT CHOCOLATE AND A PERFECTLY DECORATED GINGERBREAD MAN.

"WHY, YOU MUST BE EXHAUSTED!" SHE SAYS WITH A SMILE. "WHY DON'T YOU SIT DOWN AND ENJOY A TREAT? OH, BUT BEFORE YOU GO, COULD YOU LEND ME A HAND? I'M BAKING A NEW BATCH OF GINGERBREAD, AND I SEEM TO HAVE MISPLACED SOME OF MY INGREDIENTS!"

MRS. CLAUS HANDS YOU A RECIPE. PLACE ALL THE INGREDIENT INTO THE SPACES IN THE WORD FIT PUZZLE. AS YOU COMPLETE THE PUZZLE, YOU'LL NOTICE CERTAIN LETTERS HIGHLIGHTED IN GREEN SQUARES. ONCE YOU HAVE ALL THE LETTERS FROM THE GREEN SQUARES, REARRANGE THEM TO DISCOVER A SPECIAL WORD OR PHRASE. KEEP IT SAFE YOU WILL NEED THIS LATER IN YOUR ADVENTURE!

Homemade GINGERBREAD Cookies

- 3/4C. BUTTER
- 3/4C. BROWN SUGAR
- 3/4C. MOLASSES
- 2 TSP. CINNAMON
- 1 EGG
- 1 TSP SALT
- 1/4 TSP ALLSPICE
- 2 TSP GINGER
- 3 3/4C. FLOUR
- 1 TSP BAKING POWDER
- 1/2TSP BAKING SODA

BAKE AT 350°F FOR 8-10MINS

A SNOWY STROLL TO THE REINDEER STABLES

AFTER THE WARMTH OF MRS. CLAUS'S KITCHEN, YOU DECIDE A WALK IN THE CRISP SNOW WOULD BE REFRESHING. YOU WANDER OUTSIDE, AND AN ELF OFFERS TO GUIDE YOU TO THE REINDEER STABLES. BUT JUST AS YOU'RE ABOUT TO SET OFF, THE ELF REALIZES SOMETHING—HE'S LOST HIS HAT AND SCARF! "OH NO!" HE EXCLAIMS. "THEY'RE SOMEWHERE IN THE ELF LOST PROPERTY, MIXED UP WITH EVERYONE ELSE'S THINGS! COULD YOU HELP ME FIND MY MATCHING SET? I'D REALLY LIKE TO KEEP WARM ON OUR WALK TO THE STABLES."

THE ELF GIVES YOU A HINT: "MY SET HAS SPOTS BUT NO STRIPES!" WITH THIS CLUE, YOU'LL NEED TO IDENTIFY THE CORRECT HAT AND SCARF AMONG THE LOST ITEMS. SINCE YOU DON'T HAVE A SET EITHER, YOU DECIDE TO GRAB ONE FOR YOURSELF TO STAY WARM.

YOUR CHALLENGE:

LOOK AT THE LOST PROPERTY ITEMS AND MATCH EACH HAT WITH ITS CORRESPONDING SCARF. EACH SET HAS A UNIQUE PATTERN OR DESIGN, SO USE YOUR OBSERVATION SKILLS TO PAIR THEM CORRECTLY. MAKE NOTE OF THE LETTERS ON THE MATCHING SETS: THEY PROVIDE YOU WITH A KEYWORD AND NUMBER YOU'LL NEED LATER IN THE GAME. WHY NOT CHOOSE A SET FOR YOURSELF TO KEEP YOU WARM ON YOUR WALK TO THE REINDEER STABLES. AS A FINAL TOUCH, WHY NOT COLOR IN THE MATCHING SETS TO ADD SOME FESTIVE CHEER? USE BRIGHT COLORS TO MAKE EACH SET UNIQUE!

WITH YOUR NEW HAT AND SCARF, YOU AND THE ELF ARE READY TO HEAD TO THE REINDEER STABLES, COZY AND WARM FOR YOUR WINTER WALK.

P   N   F   U

O   K   R   I

THE REINDEER COOKIE CODE

AS YOU APPROACH THE REINDEER STALLS, YOU FIND THAT THEY'RE SECURED WITH A MAGICAL LOCK THAT CAN ONLY BE OPENED WITH A SPECIAL CODE WORD.

NEARBY, YOU SPOT JARS FILLED WITH CANDIES AND A NOTE FROM THE ELVES:

'EACH REINDEER COOKIE NEEDS 2 CANDIES FOR EYES. COUNT HOW MANY COOKIES YOU CAN MAKE FROM EACH JAR OF CANDIES, THEN MATCH THE NUMBER TO THE DECORATED CHRISTMAS STOCKINGS HANGING NEARBY.

EACH STOCKING REVEALS A WORD. ARRANGE THE WORDS IN THE CORRECT ORDER TO COMPLETE THE RIDDLE. THE ANSWER TO THIS RIDDLE WILL UNLOCK THE REINDEER STALLS!'

UNLOCKING THE MAGICAL POLISH FOR RUDOLPH'S NOSE

NOW THAT YOU HAVE ACCESS TO THE REINDEER STABLES, AN ELF ASKS IF YOU CAN HELP POLISH RUDOLPH'S NOSE. TO MAKE IT SHINE BRIGHT FOR CHRISTMAS EVE, RUDOLPH'S NOSE NEEDS A SPECIAL MAGICAL POLISH! BUT THE ELVES HAVE HIDDEN IT, AND YOU'LL NEED TO SOLVE A PUZZLE TO REVEAL IT.

YOUR CHALLENGE: COMPLETE THE CHRISTMAS PICTURE SUDOKU TO UNLOCK THE MAGICAL POLISH! CUT OUT THE CHRISTMAS PICTURE TILES. PLACE THE TILES IN THE GRID, ENSURING THAT THE SAME PICTURE DOES NOT APPEAR MORE THAN ONCE IN ANY ROW, COLUMN, OR 2X2 MINI-GRID. ONCE YOU'VE ARRANGED THE TILES CORRECTLY, THE MAGICAL POLISH WILL BE REVEALED, ALLOWING YOU TO MAKE RUDOLPH'S NOSE SPARKLE AND SHINE FOR THE BIG NIGHT!

DAY 13

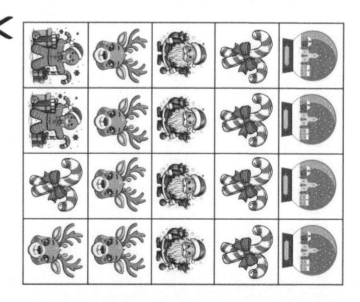

BALANCING SANTA'S SACK

JUST AS YOU'RE FINISHING UP WITH RUDOLPH, AN ELF CALLS YOU BACK TO THE WORKSHOP. "WE NEED TO PACK SANTA'S SACK, BUT IT'S TOO HEAVY!" HE EXPLAINS. TO KEEP EVERYTHING BALANCED, YOU'LL NEED TO FIGURE OUT THE WEIGHTS OF THE TOYS.

YOUR CHALLENGE: WHAT ITEM IS MISSING FORM THE LAST SET OF SCALES IN ORDER TO MAKE THEM BALANCE?

UNLOCKING THE GIFT WRAP ROOM

MRS. CLAUS IS BUSTLING AROUND, PREPARING PRESENTS, BUT SHE'S MISSING SOMETHING IMPORTANT—THE BOWS! SHE HEADS TO THE GIFT WRAP ROOM, ONLY TO REALIZE SHE'S FORGOTTEN THE PICTURE CODE NEEDED TO UNLOCK THE DOOR. SHE FOUND A NOTE WITH CLUES TO HELP HER REMEMBER, BUT WITHOUT HER READING GLASSES, SHE'S STRUGGLING TO FIGURE IT OUT. USE THE CLUES ON THE NOTE TO DISCOVER EACH DIGIT IN THE CODE AND UNLOCK THE DOOR TO THE GIFT WRAP ROOM!

ONE IMAGE IS RIGHT AND IN THE RIGHT PLACE

ONE IMAGE IS RIGHT BUT IN THE WRONG PLACE.

TWO IMAGES ARE RIGHT, BUT IN THE WRONG PLACE.

NONE OF THESE ARE CORRECT

ONE IMAGE IS RIGHT, BUT IN THE WRONG PLACE

ANSWER

16th DECORATING THE CHRISTMAS TREE

The elves are busy putting up the tree and need your help to decorate it! They ask you to connect the dots to reveal the tree and then add colors to bring it to life. But there's a hidden challenge waiting for you, too!

Your Challenge:

1. First, connect the dots in the traditional way to reveal the outline of the Christmas tree.

2. Color the tree in green. Notice that the baubles on the tree match a color key on the side. Color each bauble according to the instructions in the key.

3. The Final Challenge: Count the number of each type of bauble and record this in the key. Next, connect the dots that match these numbers in the order shown from top to bottom. This will reveal a number. Only one bauble type will cross the line—this gives you the color needed to pair with the number you've revealed.

Record the color and number and keep this information safe, as you'll need it later in your adventure!

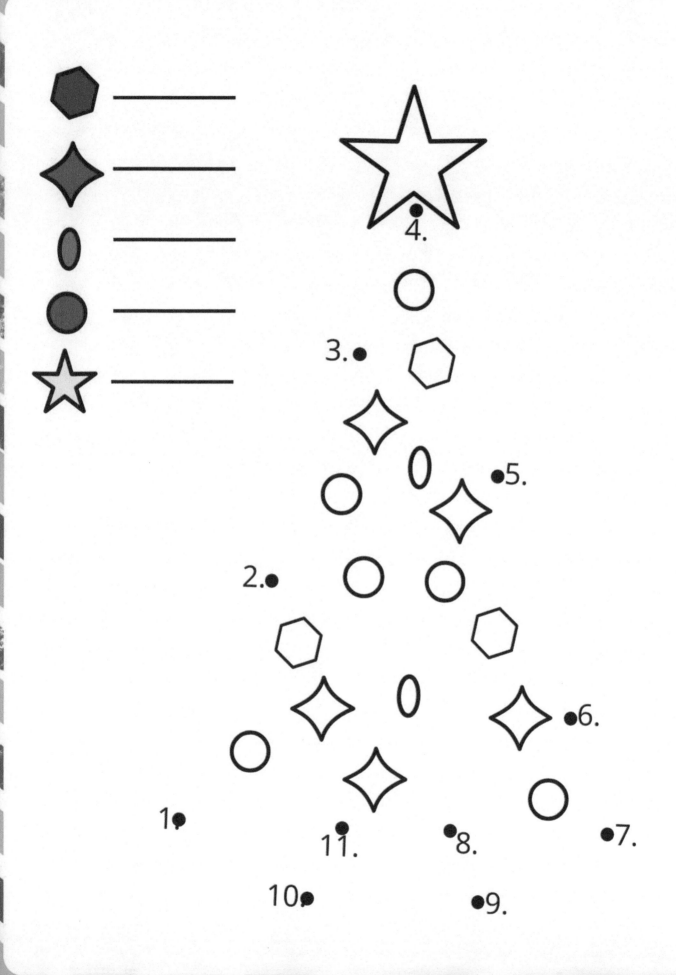

NAVIGATING SANTA'S TEST FLIGHT ROUTE

While exploring the workshop, you discover an enchanted book containing Santa's special test flight route, programmed directly into his sleigh! To keep Santa sharp, the elves have made this route challenging by adding obstacles along the way. Your task is to help Santa complete his flight by visiting each house on the map and safely reaching the finish point.

Choose the route. Begin at the square marked "Start" on the map.

Route Rules:
1. Visit All Houses.
2. Avoid Obstacles Santa's sleigh cannot pass through any square marked with an "X."
3. Each square can only be passed through once, so plan your route to ensure you can visit all houses and finish the flight at the squared marked 'End'

CALLING
THE CHIEF SLEIGH ELF

A SUDDEN BLIZZARD HAS SWEPT THROUGH THE NORTH POLE, AND SANTA'S SLEIGH HAS TAKEN A BIT OF DAMAGE. YOU NEED A SPECIAL TOOL TO FIX IT, BUT IT'S NOWHERE TO BE FOUND! THE ONLY OPTION IS TO CALL THE CHIEF SLEIGH ELF, WHO'S ON HOLIDAY, AND ASK HIM WHERE HE KEEPS IT.

IN FRONT OF YOU IS AN OLD PHONE, AND AN ELF NEARBY REMEMBERS ONE DETAIL "YOU NEED TO START AT 5, AND EACH NUMBER IN THE SEQUENCE IS A DIRECT NEIGHBOR TO THE PREVIOUS ONE. I CAN'T REMEMBER THE WHOLE NUMBER, BUT THERE'S A SEQUENCE OF ARROWS TO GUIDE YOU. PLACE YOUR FINGER ON THE NUMBER 5 ON THE PHONE. FOLLOW THE ARROWS BY MOVING YOUR FINGER TO THE NEXT NUMBER BASED ON THE DIRECTION OF EACH ARROW IN THE SEQUENCE. WRITE DOWN EACH NUMBER. ONCE YOU'VE FOLLOWED ALL THE ARROWS, YOU'LL HAVE THE TELEPHONE NUMBER NEEDED TO CALL THE CHIEF SLEIGH ELF AND GET THE TOOLS LOCATION.

ELF MAIL
DEC 12
5:00PM
NORTH POLE

↑ ← ↓ → ↓ → ↑ ↑

NORTH POLE
AIR MAIL

5 _ _ _ _ _ _ _ _

FIXING THE NORTH POLE CLOCK

Oh no! Some mischievous elves have removed the hands from the North Pole clock, putting Santa's schedule at risk! Luckily, there are five other clocks nearby, each showing a different time in a numbered sequence from 1 to 5. By figuring out the pattern between these clocks, you'll be able to set the correct time for the North Pole clock, which follows as the last one in the sequence.

Study each clock's time in order, identify the pattern, and then use it to determine the missing time for the North Pole clock!

SORTING THE GIFTS FOR SANTA'S NICE LIST

AN ELF MIX-UP MEANS THE PRESENTS ARE IN THE WRONG BOXES! IT'S ALMOST CHRISTMAS EVE, AND THE CHIEF ELF IS DOUBLE-CHECKING THE GIFTS FOR THE NEWEST BATCH OF NICE KIDS. CAN YOU WORK OUT WHICH CHILD SHOULD RECEIVE EACH GIFT USING THE CLUES BELOW?

INSTRUCTIONS:

USE THE CLUES TO FIGURE OUT WHICH GIFT BELONGS TO EACH CHILD. PLACE AN "X" IN A BOX IF IT CANNOT BE TRUE, AND A TICK (☒) IF IT'S THE CORRECT MATCH.
REMEMBER: EACH CHILD CAN RECEIVE ONLY ONE GIFT. ONCE YOU'RE CERTAIN OF A MATCH, PUT AN "X" IN THAT ROW FOR ALL OTHER CHILDREN'S NAMES TO ELIMINATE INCORRECT OPTIONS.

Puzzle Clues:

1. Sam's favorite color is blue.
2. The electric guitar was requested by Arthur.
3. The child whose favorite color is red did not want the teddy.
4. The telescope was requested by the child whose favorite color is green.
5. Anya's favorite color is not yellow, but she asked for the doll.
6. Arthur does not like the color red.
7. The child who asked for the electric guitar has yellow as their favorite color.
8. Sasha's favorite color is green, and she asked for the telescope.

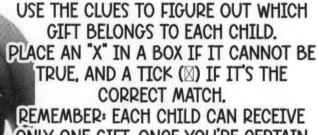

	Sam	Arthur	Anya	Sasha	Guitar	Teddy	Doll	Telescope
Blue								
Yellow								
Red								
Green								
Guitar								
Teddy								
Doll								
Telescope								

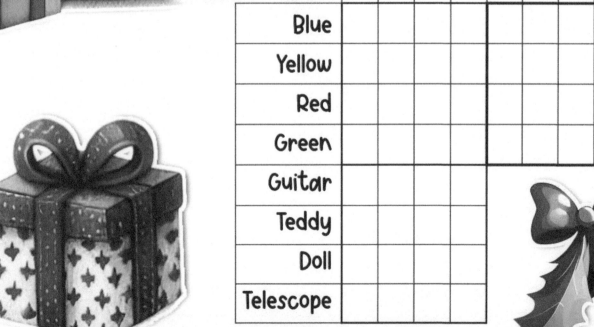

ELF QUIZ NIGHT WITH SANTA!

Team Santa

The elves have been working hard, and with so much of the pre-Christmas checklist completed, they're taking a well-deserved break! To celebrate, they're having a quiz night filled with festive puzzles and games. But this is no ordinary quiz night—Santa himself is joining in, and he's inviting you to be on his team!

Use the picture clues to identify the famous Christmas songs! Each picture represents a song title for a popular holiday tune. Once you've solved all the clues, you'll help Santa win the quiz and bring extra Christmas cheer to the North Pole!

Good luck, and remember—every answer gets you closer to a festive victory!

LIGHTING THE WAY WITH STARLIGHT

THE STARS ARE DIM TONIGHT, AND SANTA RELIES ON THEIR LIGHT TO GUIDE HIS SLEIGH. TO BRIGHTEN THE SKIES, YOU'LL NEED TO COMPLETE A SPECIAL STAR CONSTELLATION PUZZLE. BY SOLVING IT, YOU'LL HELP SANTA NAVIGATE SAFELY ON CHRISTMAS EVE!
YOUR CHALLENGE:
UNSCRAMBLE THE CHRISTMAS WORDS PROVIDED TO REVEAL FESTIVE TERMS. THESE WORDS WILL FIT INTO THE CONSTELLATION PUZZLE AND HELP FORM THE STARS SANTA NEEDS TO LIGHT HIS WAY.
WE'VE ADDED A CLUES AND A FEW LETTERS TO GIVE YOU A HELPFUL START!
ONCE THE PUZZLE IS COMPLETE, THE STARS WILL SHINE BRIGHTLY, LIGHTING UP THE SKY AND HELPING SANTA FIND HIS WAY.

FUELING UP FOR THE BIG NIGHT!

Santa's getting ready to deliver presents all over the world, which takes a lot of energy! Even with the drinks and snacks left by kind children, he needs a boost to keep him going all night long. Mrs. Claus and the elves have been busy baking up a storm to give Santa the energy he needs!

Your Challenge: Help Mrs. Claus and the elves by matching the completed cookie sheets to their mixing bowls based on the sum of their ingredients. When matched correctly, the letters on the mixing bowls will reveal an important word or phrase you'll need for tomorrow's final preparations! With your help, Santa will have the energy he needs to spread joy around the world!

FUELING UP FOR THE BIG NIGHT

STARTING SANTA'S SLEIGH FOR CHRISTMAS EVE!

It's finally Christmas Eve, and Santa's sleigh is packed, polished, and ready for takeoff! But there's one last hitch: the chief mechanic elf is snowed in at Bondi Beach and hasn't been able to call in the boost start code needed to power Santa's sleigh for the whole night!

Luckily, he left behind a clue in the form of a color puzzle to help. By gathering the items and stars you've collected throughout your adventure, you'll be able to crack the final code and save Christmas!

Gather each colored item and place it in the order shown on the color key. Do the Math for each pair to reveal a 4-digit code. Insert Your Magical Stars to give the sleigh the final boost it needs.

Once everything is in place, the sleigh will be fully powered, ready for Santa to deliver joy to children around the world. Thanks to your help, Christmas is saved!

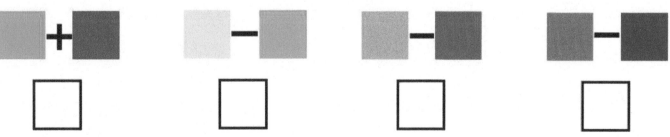

Day 1: The Magic of the Snow Globe

Instructions for Parents:

- Encourage children to carefully examine each snowflake, pointing out that while some may look similar, only two are identical. For younger children, you may want to help by narrowing down options, counting points on each snowflake, or checking shapes until they find the matching pair. Keep the excitement up as this puzzle begins the magical adventure!
- Also hand the children the Codex Wheel to solve the bonus code.

Elf Tip (for Younger Players):
"Sometimes, snowflakes look very similar, but only two are exactly the same. Look closely at the shapes and count each point on the snowflakes. If you're unsure, ask a grown-up for help, and keep trying!"

Answer - On Right

Story Extension for Parents:

As soon as you find the two identical snowflakes, the snow globe begins to glow even brighter, and a magical warmth surrounds you. In a swirl of sparkling snow, you feel yourself gently lifted off your feet and carried through a flurry of shimmering flakes!

When the snow settles, you find yourself standing in a snowy wonderland—the North Pole! Snow-covered trees twinkle with frost, and tiny lights flicker in the distance, guiding you toward a cozy glow just ahead. You realize that Santa's Workshop is nearby, waiting for you to make your way through the wintry landscape.

Then, a friendly elf appears, bundled up with a scarf and mittens. "Welcome to the North Pole!" he says, his voice bright with excitement. "Santa's Workshop is just down this hill, but there are a few snowy challenges along the way! Each day, a new task will help bring you closer to the workshop— and to Santa himself! Let's get moving, and remember, every puzzle you solve brings us one step closer to Christmas Eve!"

With a smile and a wave, the elf points you toward the path, and your magical journey to the workshop begins!

Day 2: Navigating the North Pole

Instructions for Parents:

- For younger children, explain how to follow directions by looking at each constellation, focusing on the arrows and counting the stars to determine how many steps to move and in which direction. You may want to guide them by tracing each step on the map to show them how to travel in the correct direction. Using a small coin or marker can help them keep track of their moves as they work out the route to Santa's workshop.

Elf Tip (for Younger Players):
"Each constellation in the sky has arrows that show you which direction to go. Follow the arrows carefully, and count the stars in each one—that's how many spaces you need to move in that direction on the map. Take it step-by-step, and you'll find the right path!"

Answer - On right

Story Extension for Parents:

With a newfound sense of direction, you see a soft glow lighting up in the distance—it's the way to Santa's Workshop! The constellations have revealed a path to guide you through the snowy landscape, and your heart races with excitement at the wonders that await.

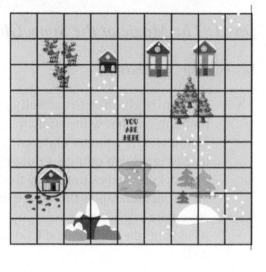

The journey won't be easy; you'll need to venture through an enchanted woodland and cross a frozen lake before reaching the workshop. Just as you're picturing the adventure ahead, an elf waves to you from the edge of the trees.

"Fantastic work finding the way!" he calls out. "Ahead lies a magical woodland, and beyond that, a frozen lake. Follow the clues carefully, and you'll reach Santa's Workshop in no time!"

With a smile and a sense of adventure, you step forward, feeling the crunch of snow beneath your boots. The path to Santa's Workshop awaits, filled with surprises and holiday cheer!

Day 3: The Enchanted Woodland

Instructions for Parents:

- This puzzle may require a few tries to find the correct route, so consider printing a spare copy and having your child use a pencil to make it easy to erase any mistakes.
- If your child is having trouble, suggest they try working backward from the endpoint, as this can sometimes help reveal the correct path.
- Once the route is found, remind your child to look carefully at the letters passed along the way, as they form an important phrase.
- Once the puzzle is complete, hand your child the GREEN tree marked with the number 8, reminding them to hold onto it for the journey's end. An elf hints that this special item is important and should be kept safe, though its purpose will be revealed later.
- **Elf Tip** (for Younger Players):
  "Paths can be tricky! Try working backward if you're having trouble. And remember, the letters along the way spell out a phrase you'll need later—keep it safe!"

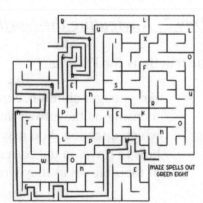

MAZE SPELLS OUT GREEN EIGHT

Answer - GREEN EIGHT Picture on right

Story Extension for Parents:

After carefully solving the maze and finding your way through the twists and turns of the enchanted woodland, you finally step out into an open, snowy landscape. You look ahead, and in the distance, you see the glow of Santa's workshop doors standing tall and welcoming, adorned with twinkling lights.

As you take in the view, the friendly elf appears once again, smiling brightly. "You made it through the forest! You're getting closer to Santa's workshop!" he says, handing you a small green tree ornament with the number "8" on it. "Keep this safe—it may come in handy later."

With excitement growing, you tuck the ornament away and continue your journey, one step closer to Santa's magical workshop.

Day 4: Crossing the Frozen Lake

Instructions for Parents:

- For younger children, consider marking the first stepping stone to demonstrate how the overlapping images guide them across. This can help them understand how to use the coordinates to find the safe path.
- Encourage your child to look at each symbol along the side of the lake and find where the symbols intersect on the grid to reveal a safe stepping stone. This will allow them to hop safely from one stone to the next.
- **Note:** Do not provide the codex for this challenge. Although it uses similar symbols, it works differently and may confuse the children.

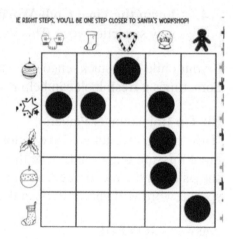

Elf Tip (for Younger Players):
"To find each safe stepping stone, look at the pictures along the top row and the side row of the lake. Find one picture from the top and one from the side, and follow each into the lake. Where the two pictures meet, you'll find a safe spot to step. Keep following these matching spots to cross safely!"

Answer - On right

Story Extension for Parents:

With careful steps and a little Christmas magic, you hop from one safe stone to the next, making your way across the frozen lake. Each step brings a surge of excitement as you near the other side.

When you finally reach solid ground, you look up and gasp. In the distance, you think you can see the grand doors of Santa's Workshop, standing tall and welcoming, adorned with twinkling lights and evergreen garlands. The workshop glows warmly in the snowy landscape, inviting you to come closer.

The friendly elf from before appears at your side once again, beaming with pride. "Well done!" he says. "You've crossed the lake, and the doors of Santa's Workshop are just ahead! Let's go; there's much to see and do inside!"

Filled with joy and anticipation, you take a deep breath and start toward the grand doors, ready for the wonders that await you in Santa's Workshop.

Parent Instructions

This puzzle is a bit more challenging, as it requires logical thinking and pattern recognition. Encourage your child to take their time and approach it step-by-step. You can cut out the wheels if you think the child would find this easier we do provide a pair of blank locks in the Extra kit should you wish to do this and it also enables you to enter the traffic light output letters for each word.

1. **Identify the Missing Letters:** Help your child examine each word on the left side of the lock and identify which letters are missing. Each word is missing three letters, so finding these should be their first step.

2. **Align the Wheels Carefully:** Once they've figured out the missing letters, assist them in setting the lock wheels so the letters are positioned at 1, 2, and 3. The first word is MAN.

3. **Check the Outputs Together:** After aligning the wheels, point out the output sections at the bottom (red, orange, and green). These outputs will display the letters at the bottom of each wheel.

4. **Form the Final Code Word:** Remind your child to read the outputs in sequence to form the new six-letter word. This will be the magic code to open the workshop doors!

If your child gets stuck, encourage them to go back and double-check each missing letter. Sometimes a fresh look can help reveal the solution!

Elf Tip (for Younger Players):
"Hey there, Adventurer! Take a close look at the words—each one is missing three letters. Find those missing letters and rotate the wheels until they appear in positions 1, 2, and 3. Watch what shows up in the red, orange, and green slots at the bottom. If you line everything up just right, a special word will appear to open the door!"

Answer - JOYFUL

Story Extension for Parents:

With a final look at the keypad, you enter the missing number, and suddenly, the grand doors of Santa's Workshop begin to glow. They swing open slowly, revealing a cozy warmth and the cheerful hum of elves at work inside.

As you step through the doors, you're greeted by rows of bustling workstations, where elves are crafting toys, wrapping gifts, and preparing treats. The air is filled with the scent of pine and peppermint, and everywhere you look, twinkling lights cast a magical glow.

The friendly elf beams at you. "Welcome to Santa's Workshop! There are many exciting tasks ahead, and each one brings us closer to making this Christmas unforgettable. Let's get started— there's lots to do!"

You step further inside, filled with excitement for the wonders you'll see and the tasks you'll help complete in the days to come.

Day 6: The Magical Toy Sorter

Parent Instructions:

- For younger children, you may wish to cut out the pieces ahead of time or print a spare copy of the puzzle in case the pieces need to be re-cut.
- Once the puzzle is complete, hand your child the ORANGE basketball marked with the number 6.

Elf Tip (for Younger Players):
"This puzzle is simple! Just try to make the picture look right, and the correct code will reveal itself. Look carefully at Santa and the reindeer to see where each piece should go."

Answer - ORANGE 6 Picture on right

Story Extension for Parents:

With careful hands, you place the last piece into the picture, restoring the image of Santa and his reindeer. Instantly, the toy sorter whirs to life! Toys begin moving smoothly along the conveyor belts again, with each gift magically finding its place.

The elf grins with gratitude. "You've done it! The sorter is back on track, and thanks to you, the elves can keep working their Christmas magic. Now, as promised, I'll show you more of the workshop floor!"

He hands you an orange basketball with the number "6" written on it. "This is a little keepsake for your help today. Be sure to hold on to it!"

He then leads you deeper into the heart of the workshop, where elves are hammering, painting, and wrapping gifts with incredible speed. Shelves overflow with colorful toys and twinkling decorations, while holiday music fills the air.

With each step, you're filled with wonder at the magic and joy that goes into every Christmas gift. The journey continues, and you can't wait to see what you'll discover next!

Day 7: The Missing Naughty and Nice List

Parent Instructions:

- Encourage your child to color in the image after they find the list, especially if they enjoy coloring or if they complete the puzzle quickly. This adds an extra creative element to their adventure.

Elf Tip (for Younger Players):
"To find the Naughty and Nice List, try looking around the image in a pattern—maybe go clockwise and work your way toward the center. This way, you'll be sure to check every part of the workshop and won't miss anything important!"

Answer - on Right

Story Extension for Parents:

After carefully searching each corner of the workshop, you finally spot the book mixed in with a pile of toys. With a sigh of relief, you pull it out—Santa's Naughty and Nice List! The head elf's eyes light up as he takes the list from you, clutching it with joy.

"You've saved Christmas preparations!" he says with a grin. "Santa would be lost without this list. Now we can keep track of all the boys and girls around the world and make sure each gift finds its way to the right home."

He pats your shoulder and gives a grateful nod. "You're proving to be a real helper here in the workshop! We couldn't do this without you. Now that the list is back where it belongs, there's still more to be done. Let's keep going—Christmas Eve will be here before we know it!"

With a happy heart, you continue through the bustling workshop, ready to tackle the next task and make sure Christmas is magical for everyone!

Day 8: Lighting Up the Workshop

Parent Instructions:

- This puzzle may be more challenging, especially for younger children. Here are some ways to help:
    - **Start by demonstrating**: Use the example red crystal to show how the light beam changes direction when it hits a mirror. Explain that each mirror turns the light 90 degrees.
    - **Use a ruler for guidance**: Place a ruler along the path to help your child see how the beam should move from mirror to mirror.
    - **Break it down step-by-step**: Go slowly, helping your child track each movement of the light one at a time. Encourage them to test a crystal by following the path from one mirror to the next.
    - **Check along the way**: Encourage your child to note if the light beam ends too soon or goes in the wrong direction. This will help them rule out incorrect crystals.
- Once the puzzle is complete, hand your child the YELLOW Crystal marked with the number 3.

Elf Tip (for Younger Players):
"Take a look at the red crystal example. Watch how the light beam changes direction each time it hits a mirror. Use a ruler to follow the path of each crystal carefully—start at the beginning, and every time you hit a mirror, turn your ruler 90 degrees. The correct crystal will keep the light going all the way!"

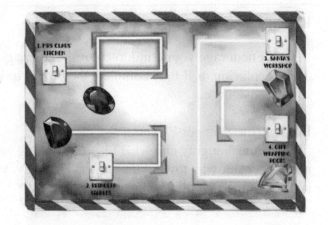

Answer - RED 3 Picture on Right

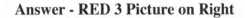

Story Extension for Parents:

After carefully tracing the light path and choosing the right crystal, you press it back into place. In an instant, a warm glow fills the workshop as the lights spring to life, casting a festive glow on everything around you. The entire room seems to sparkle with magic, and the elves cheer with joy.

The head elf claps you on the back, his eyes shining with excitement. "You've done it! The workshop is brightly lit and ready for the busy days ahead. Santa's elves can now work in full light, thanks to you!"

He hands you a yellow crystal with the number "3" written on it and says, "Be sure to remember the color of this crystal and the light switch number. Trust me, it'll be important later on!"

Filled with pride, you look around at the bustling workshop, now glowing with holiday warmth. With every task you complete, you feel closer to helping Santa get ready for Christmas Eve!

Day 9: Fixing the Conveyor Belt

Parent Instructions:

- For younger children, consider cutting out the gear pieces ahead of time (we provide a larger copy to cut at the end of the pack) to make it easier for them to try each piece on the broken gear. Older children may prefer to cut out the pieces themselves, but cutting should not be required to solve the puzzle.
- To help your child understand how cogs (gears) work, explain that each gear turns the one next to it in the opposite direction. So, if one gear turns clockwise, the one it touches will turn counterclockwise, and vice versa.
- This pattern continues down the line of gears. For example, if you want the conveyor belt to move to the right, look at the direction each gear would need to turn to make that happen. You can use this knowledge to help your child figure out which direction to turn the handle to get the belt moving forward.
- For a hands-on demonstration, consider using bottle caps or small objects as "gears" to show how they turn each other in opposite directions.

Elf Tip (for Younger Players):
"Try fitting each gear piece into the broken spot on the conveyor belt. Keep testing the shapes until you find the one that completes the gear perfectly!"

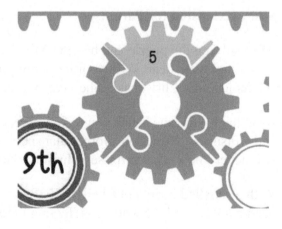

Answer - You would turn the handle counter clockwise to move the conveyor belt forward as the only cog that connect to the belt this will mean it move forward to the right. This setup ensures that filling in the missing part is necessary to complete the mechanism and control the belt's direction.

Story Extension for Parents:

With a bit of trial and error, you carefully place the missing gear piece, and suddenly, the conveyor belt hums back to life! Toys begin to move along the belt again, each one getting closer to being wrapped, packed, and ready for Christmas Eve.

The nearby elves cheer as they get back to work, grateful for your quick thinking. The head elf grins and nods approvingly. "Wonderful job! You're really getting the hang of this workshop business. Thanks to you, the toys will be ready in time!"

With a feeling of pride, you watch the conveyor belt smoothly roll forward, and you know you're making a real difference here. There's still more to do, and the elves can't wait to see what else you can help with!

Day 10: A Visit with Mrs. Claus

Parent Instructions:

- Younger children may find the anagram challenging. To help, you can write the numbers 1 through 9 in **words** (e.g., "one," "two," "three") and colours on a spare sheet of paper. This can guide them in matching the letters from the green squares to spell the phrase "brown nine."
- Once the puzzle is complete, hand your child the BROWN gingerbread man marked with the number 9.

Elf Tip (for Younger Players):
"If the special phrase seems tricky, try writing down numbers as words on another sheet, like 'one,' 'two,' and so on. Match each letter from the green squares to these words—it might help you solve the puzzle more easily!"

Answer - BROWN NINE Picture on right

Story Extension for Parents:

After solving the puzzle and helping Mrs. Claus with her ingredients, she claps her hands in delight. "Oh, thank you, dear! With your help, my gingerbread recipe is back on track, and the kitchen smells just like Christmas!" She gives you a warm smile, her eyes twinkling with gratitude.

As a thank-you, she hands you a gingerbread man with the number "9" written on it. She leans in and whispers, "Now, don't forget that special phrase you discovered. It may come in handy later—you never know what surprises Christmas has in store!"

With a satisfied heart and a belly full of cocoa and gingerbread, you bid Mrs. Claus goodbye and head back toward the workshop, feeling ready for whatever magical task comes next.

Day 11: A Snowy Stroll to the Reindeer Stables

Parent Instructions:

- This puzzle may be challenging for younger children. Adding colors to each hat and scarf set in advanced can make it easier for them to match up the patterns. For example, color each matching set with the same color to help them recognize pairs more easily.
- Remind them to take note of the letters on each matching set, which spell out an important code when written in the order of the top row.
- Once the puzzle is complete, hand your child the PINK glove marked with the number 4.

Elf Tip (for Younger Players):
"Look closely at each hat and scarf. Pay attention to patterns—some have spots, some have stripes, and some have both. Match the ones that look the same, and don't forget to note the letters on each pair. They'll spell out something special!"

Answer - PINK FOUR Picture on right. Elf set is F-O

Story Extension for Parents:

After carefully matching each hat and scarf, you finally find the elf's missing set—it's the one with spots but no stripes! With a sigh of relief, the elf wraps up in his cozy hat and scarf, looking ready for the cold winter walk.

As a token of thanks, he hands you a pink glove with the number "4" written on it. He grins and says, "Thank you so much! Now, we're both ready for the reindeer stables.

You slip on your own matching set and follow the elf, bundled up warmly as you head toward the stables. The snow crunches under your feet, and you can't wait to meet Santa's reindeer. Each step brings you closer to the next magical part of your North Pole adventure!

Day 12: The Reindeer Cookie Code

Parent Instructions:

- Encourage your child to tackle this puzzle in stages. First, have them count the candies in each jar and write down the total. Next, help them divide the candies to find out how many cookies can be made from each jar (each cookie needs 2 candies for eyes). Finally, match the number of cookies to the stockings to reveal the words for the riddle, which will lead to the code word.

Elf Tip (for Younger Players):
"Take it one step at a time! Start by counting the candies in each jar. Then, divide the candies to see how many reindeer cookies you can make (each one needs 2 candies for eyes). Find the matching stocking with the number you've worked out—it'll give you a special letter!"

Answer - Buttons and a carrot, I'm cold and round? - SNOWMAN is code word.

Story Extension for Parents:

After counting candies, calculating cookies, and piecing together the letters, you finally reveal the magic word! You say it out loud SNOWMAN, and with a soft *click*, the lock on the reindeer stalls releases.

The stable doors swing open, and you're greeted by the happy sounds of Santa's reindeer, each one eagerly awaiting their Christmas Eve flight. The elf beams with pride. "Thanks to you, the reindeer are ready for their final preparations! Soon, they'll be soaring across the sky."

With a warm smile, you reach out to pat the nose of one of the reindeer, feeling the excitement build for the big night. The next part of your adventure awaits, and you're ready for whatever magical task comes next!

Day 13: Unlocking the Magical Polish for Rudolph's Nose

Parent Instructions:

- For younger children, consider cutting out the picture tiles ahead of time to make it easier for them to focus on arranging them in the grid.
- Encourage them to start with the Gingerbread tiles, as there are fewer options for spaces, which can help guide them. Remind them of the Sudoku rule: no repeated pictures in any row, column, or 3x2 mini-grid.
- Once they complete the puzzle, they can choose to glue down the pieces if they'd like to make it permanent, though this is optional.

Elf Tip (for Younger Players):
"Try placing the Gingerbread tiles first since there are fewer spaces they can go in—that might make the puzzle easier. Remember, each row, column, and 3x2 square should only have one of each picture!"

Answer - On right

Story Extension for Parents:

With the picture puzzle complete, the magical polish is revealed, shimmering in its jar on a nearby shelf. An elf hands it to you with a grin and says, "Great work! Now, Rudolph's nose can shine as bright as a star on Christmas Eve!"

You carefully polish Rudolph's nose, watching as it glows even brighter with each gentle rub. Soon, his nose is beaming with a magical red light, ready to guide Santa's sleigh through any stormy weather.

The other reindeer stomp their hooves in excitement, and Rudolph gives a happy snort, proud of his sparkling nose. The elf winks at you. "Thanks to you, Rudolph is all set! Now the team is ready to take on the skies!"

With a feeling of pride, you say goodbye to the reindeer and head back to the workshop, eager to see what comes next in your adventure.

Day 14: Balancing Santa's Sack

Parent Instructions:

- For younger children, using physical items to demonstrate weight balance can be very helpful. If you have access to scales, use small items like blocks or toys to show how weights can be balanced. If not, gather four teddies and some balls or blocks to demonstrate how different items compare in weight.

Elf Tip (for Younger Players):
"Look at how many balls one teddy weighs. This will help you figure out what's missing from the last scales!"

Answer - 1 Ball is needed to balance the scales.

Story Extension for Parents:

With a careful eye and some quick calculations, you add the missing Baseball to the scale—and it balances perfectly! The elf gives a cheer as the scales level out, and Santa's sack is now packed just right.

"Thanks to you, Santa's sack is balanced and ready for the big night!" the elf exclaims. "We couldn't do it without your sharp mind and quick thinking."

You watch as the elves securely close up the sack, knowing that it's now perfectly balanced for Santa's journey. With each challenge, you're getting closer to helping Santa make this Christmas magical for everyone!

With pride and excitement, you head off, wondering what the next task will be in this incredible adventure.

Day 15: Unlocking the Gift Wrap Room

Parent Instructions:

This logic puzzle encourages your child to use reasoning and deduction skills to figure out the correct sequence of images. Each clue gives hints about which images are correct and whether they're in the right position.

How to Guide Your Child:

1. **Explain the Clues:** Help your child understand that each clue provides information about which images are correct and whether they are in the right spot. For example:

   - "One image is right and in the right place" means that one of the images is correct and is in the correct box in the sequence.
   - "One image is right but in the wrong place" suggests an image is part of the solution but is not currently in the correct box.

2. **Work Step-by-Step:** Encourage your child to start with the clues that give the most information and eliminate possibilities. They can try to place images and adjust based on each clue.

3. **Use a Process of Elimination:** Encourage your child to use each clue to eliminate images that don't fit or to try out placements that satisfy each condition.

4. **Trial and Error:** This puzzle may require a bit of trial and error. Remind your child that it's okay to try different combinations until the correct one is found. You can always give them the position of one image to help them solve it themselves for example tell them the Gingerbread man is in position 2.

5. **Check the Final Answer:** Once they think they've found the correct combination, review the clues together to make sure each one is satisfied by the answer.

Elf Tip (for younger players): "Take it slow and look at each clue carefully. You're trying to find the right order for the images, like a Christmas puzzle! If you need help, ask a grown-up to go through each clue with you."

Answer - Bauble, Gingerbread man & Gem.

Story Extension for Parents:

After carefully working through each clue, you finally unlock the door to the gift wrap room. Mrs. Claus beams with delight, clapping her hands. "Oh, thank you, dear! Now I can add bows to each gift and make them look just perfect for Christmas!"

You watch as Mrs. Claus gathers rolls of colorful ribbons and sparkly bows, getting everything ready to make each present extra special. She winks at you and says, "With your help, Christmas is looking brighter and brighter!"

Feeling accomplished, you head back to the workshop, knowing you're one step closer to making sure every detail for Christmas Eve is just right.

Day 16: Decorating the Christmas Tree

Parent Instructions:

*   Encourage younger children to take it step-by-step. Have coloring supplies ready, and help them locate the numbers to connect the dots. Guide them to color the tree and baubles using the key on the page.
*   For the final part, support them in counting each type of bauble, then have them connect the dots in the order shown. This should reveal the number 3, with only the red diamond bauble crossed. The answer is "red 3."
*   Once the puzzle is complete, hand your child the RED Bauble marked with the number 3.

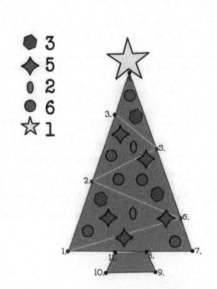

Elf Tip (for Younger Players):
"Go step-by-step—first connect the dots to reveal the tree, then use the key to color each bauble. Count each type of bauble and connect the dots to reveal a secret number. Only one bauble will cross your line—this is your answer!"

Answer - RED 3 picture on Right

Story Extension for Parents:

After connecting the dots, coloring in the tree, and revealing the hidden number, the Christmas tree sparkles with festive cheer! The elves clap with delight as they admire your work. "It's perfect!" they exclaim. "Now, with such a beautiful tree, Santa's Workshop is truly ready for Christmas!"

They hand you a small, glittering red ornament with the number 3 engraved on it. "Keep this safe," one elf whispers with a twinkle in his eye. "You'll understand its importance soon!"

With the workshop glowing from the decorated tree, you feel the joy of the season warming you from the inside out. The adventure continues, and you can't wait to see what comes next!

Day 17: Navigating Santa's Test Flight Route

Parent Instructions:

- This puzzle may be challenging for younger children, so take time to discuss the map with them. Use a coin or counter to show how Santa's sleigh can move from one spot to the next, avoiding obstacles. Let them try a few practice moves, and encourage them to record the final route in the magical handbook, so Santa can follow it later.

Elf Tip (for Younger Players):
"Use a coin or counter to trace Santa's path. Start at the sleigh and plan each move, but watch out for obstacles! Once you find the right route, jot it down in the magical handbook."

Answer - On right

Story Extension for Parents:

After carefully plotting Santa's route and marking it in the magical handbook, you feel a surge of pride. You've just completed Santa's test flight path! An elf appears beside you, clapping his hands with excitement.

"Fantastic work! Santa will be impressed by your careful planning. Thanks to you, he'll know just how to navigate his flight on Christmas Eve," the elf says, grinning.

He hands you a tiny star-shaped charm as a token of appreciation. "This charm is a special reminder of the path you've created. Keep it with you—you never know when a bit of starlight might come in handy!"

With Santa's route safely recorded, you feel ready for the next magical task, knowing that Christmas Eve is one step closer to being a success!

Day 18: Calling the Chief Sleigh Elf

Parent Instructions:

- Encourage your child to use a coin or counter to trace their steps as they follow the instructions on the map. Since they practiced a similar puzzle earlier, this should feel familiar, but remind them to record each number as they go along to keep track of their moves. A pencil could also be used to draw the route you take across the keypad.

Elf Tip (for Younger Players):
"Use a coin to mark each step as you follow the directions. Be sure to write down the numbers as you go—you'll need them to complete the puzzle!"

Answer - 521-458-963

Story Extension for Parents:

After carefully following each arrow and dialing the completed code into the old-fashioned phone, the line crackles, and you hear a cheerful voice—it's the Chief Sleigh Elf! You can hear the sounds of waves and laughter in the background.

"Well done! I knew you'd figure it out!" he says with a chuckle. "I'm here on Bondi Beach, enjoying a bit of sunshine and catching some waves. Quite the contrast from the North Pole, eh?"

With a warm laugh, he adds, "Now, I may be far from the workshop, but I can still help you find the tool you need. Check the toolbox beside Santa's sleigh—it's tucked in there safe and sound!"

With his guidance, you know exactly where to find the missing tool. Each step brings you closer to preparing Santa's sleigh, and you're filled with excitement as the big night approaches!

Day 19: Fixing the North Pole Clock

Parent Instructions:

- This puzzle is all about recognizing patterns in time. If your child isn't yet familiar with telling time, focus on the shorter hand and help them see where it points to identify each hour. Encourage them to write down these numbers in the sequence shown by the clocks.
- You may also want to draw the long hand on the clock for them and ask what number should come next. Show them how to add the hour hand step-by-step to complete the missing time.

Elf Tip (for Younger Players):
"Look at each clock and see where the short hand points—this shows you the hour. Write each hour down in the order the clocks are numbered and see if you can spot a pattern!"

Answer - The hour hand on each clock moves forward by 2 hours in sequence: 12, 2, 4, 6, 8, which means the next hour will be 10. The minute hand moves forward by 15 minutes with each clock: 00, 15, 30, 45, 00, so the next minute will be 15. Together, this makes the time 10:15.

Story Extension for Parents:

After carefully figuring out the pattern, you place the hands on the North Pole clock to 10 O'clock, setting it to the correct time. The clock chimes softly 10 times, and you breathe a sigh of relief—Santa's schedule is back on track!

An elf appears, grinning from ear to ear. "Thank you! Now Santa will be right on time for every stop on Christmas Eve. We couldn't have done it without your help!"

With the North Pole clock ticking away, you feel a surge of excitement. The workshop is almost ready, and you're one step closer to making sure Santa's big night goes off without a hitch. Smiling, you head off to see what's next, ready for the adventure ahead.

Day 20: Sorting the Gifts for Santa's Nice List

Parent Instructions:

- This is a logic puzzle where each answer is unique. Encourage younger children to approach it step-by-step, discussing each clue and helping them mark answers they're sure about.
- Remind them to eliminate other options once a choice is confirmed, and suggest using a pencil for easy corrections or have an extra copy printed just in case.

Elf Tip (for Younger Players):
"Take it one step at a time! Each clue gives you information to help you match the gifts. Once you know which gift is for one child, cross off that option for the others."

Answer - On right

Child	Favorite Color	Requested Gift
Sam	Blue	Teddy
Arthur	Yellow	Electric Guitar
Anya	Red	Doll
Sasha	Green	Telescope

Story Extension for Parents:

After carefully working through the clues and matching each gift to the correct child, you finally have everything sorted. The chief elf beams with joy, clapping his hands in relief.

"Thank you! Thanks to you, each gift will go to the right child, just as Santa planned. Now, every present on the Nice List is ready to bring joy on Christmas morning!"

He hands you a little golden star as a token of appreciation. "This star is a symbol of all the good you've done in the workshop. Keep it with you as we move closer to Christmas Eve!"

With a warm feeling of accomplishment, you look forward to the final preparations, knowing you've helped make Christmas magical for children around the world.

Day 21: Elf Quiz Night with Santa!

Parent Instructions:

- Encourage children to simply 'say what they see' for each puzzle. This can help them recognize familiar Christmas phrases and songs. If a particular phrase is tricky, try playing the song as they work it out. Playing Christmas songs daily as they solve each puzzle can also help them become familiar with common holiday phrases.

Elf Tip (for Younger Players):
"Each picture in the quiz represents a well-known Christmas song or saying. Look carefully and try to name what you see—it'll help you figure out the answer!"

Answer - Little Donkey, Jingle Bells, Dreaming of a white Christmas & O Christmas Tree.

Story Extension for Parents:

After successfully helping Santa's team with the quiz, everyone claps and cheers. Santa himself gives a hearty laugh and pats you on the back, saying, "Well done! You've got a great eye for Christmas clues—I couldn't have done it without you!"

The elves bring out a plate of holiday treats, and Santa raises his hot chocolate in a toast. "To our newest helper and to a magical Christmas Eve! With your help, everything is falling perfectly into place."

The warmth and joy of the evening fill you with excitement as the countdown to Christmas grows shorter. You feel honored to be a part of the North Pole festivities, and with each task, you're helping make the holiday season extra special!

Day 22: Lighting the Way with Starlight

Parent Instructions:

- Make sure children understand they need to unscramble the letters in each box to form Christmas words. For younger children, work through the words verbally together, then help them write out the correct words. They can then copy these into the puzzle to complete the constellation.
- Once the puzzle is complete, hand your child the PURPLE GIFT marked with the number 1.

Elf Tip (for Younger Players):
"Here is a clue for each one

Corals - Sung at Christmas?

his leg - Carries Santa and gifts on Christmas eve

Reed Rein - There are 9 famous ones

Net Press - Things given at Christmas

Imp nice - Christmas pastry

Casual Ants - Also called St Nick

Tick song - Hung over fireplace

Big Gardener - Something houses at Christmas are made from"

Answer - On Right

Story Extension for Parents:

After carefully filling in each word and completing the constellation puzzle, you watch as the stars twinkle to life in the night sky. The once-dim heavens now glow with a beautiful, festive light, illuminating Santa's flight path.

An elf appears, smiling proudly, and hands you a small gift with the number "1" written on it. "You've done it! This gift is a token of thanks for lighting Santa's way. With your help, he'll have the brightest starlight to guide him on Christmas Eve!"

You tuck the gift safely away, feeling a sense of wonder knowing that your efforts have helped light Santa's way. As the stars shine down, filling the sky with warmth and magic, you feel even more excited, knowing Christmas Eve is just around the corner.

Day 23: Fueling Up for the Big Night!

Parent Instructions:

- For younger children, guide them step-by-step. Start by asking them to count the cookies on each tray and record the number. Then, have them do the simple math for each bowl to find the correct sums. Finally, match the numbers to reveal the hidden phrase. Encourage them to go slowly and check each step to make sure everything matches up.
- Once the puzzle is complete, hand your child the BLUE Cookie marked with the number 5.

Elf Tip (for Younger Players):
"First, count the cookies on each tray. Then, do a little math for each bowl, and match up the numbers to uncover the secret phrase!"

Answer - BLUE FIVE

Story Extension for Parents:

After you help Mrs. Claus and the elves match the cookie sheets to their bowls, Mrs. Claus smiles warmly and hands you a special blue cookie with the number "5" written on it. "Keep this safe," she says with a wink. "It's a little surprise for later!"

With Santa's energy-boosting treats ready, you know he'll have all he needs to complete his journey around the world. The workshop is bustling with excitement, and you feel a sense of pride knowing you've helped fuel Santa's mission!

Day 24: Starting Santa's Sleigh for Christmas Eve!

Parent Instructions:

- For younger children, lay out the collected objects from previous days in the order indicated by the color key. Guide them through matching each item with the color code, then help them do the math for each pair to find the final numbers needed. This step-by-step approach will make it easier to unlock the sleigh.
- There is a bonus code to decipher too on this day with your codex wheel.

Elf Tip (for Younger Players):
"Place each item in the order of the color key and add the numbers as shown to reveal the final code. Remember, each number is a piece of the Christmas magic!"

Answer - 9538

Story Extension for Parents:

As you place each item in the correct spot and do the final calculations, the sleigh hums to life, glowing with a magical energy! You insert the three stars, and the sleigh shines even brighter. The elves cheer, and Santa climbs into the sleigh, grinning from ear to ear.

With a warm laugh, Santa looks down at you and says, "Thank you, my friend. I couldn't have done it without you! Now, let's make this a Christmas to remember."

With a twinkle in his eye, he gives you a wink, then takes off into the sky, his sleigh trailing stardust as it soars through the night. You've done it—you've saved Christmas!

Codex Assembly Instructions

1 - Cut out both wheels along the black outline.

2 - Use a sharp point or pencil to make a hole in the centre of each wheel (marked with a dot).

3 - Join the wheels using a split pin. If you don't have a split pin, place the smaller wheel on top and rotate it on a flat surface.

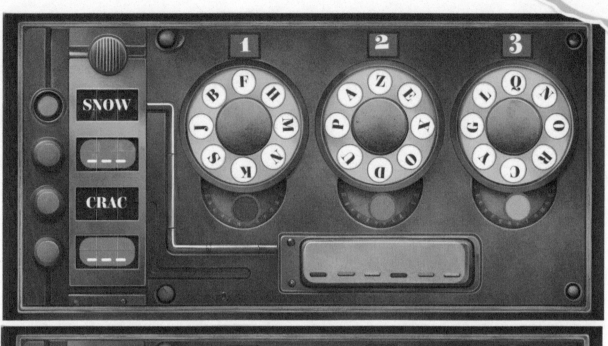

Made in the USA
Monee, IL
02 December 2024

72207825R00044